THIS WALKER BOOK BELONGS TO:

_____

_____

_____

For Oscar

First published 1994 by Walker Books Ltd
87 Vauxhall Walk, London SE11 5HJ

This edition published 2006

2 4 6 8 10 9 7 5 3 1

© 1994, 2006 Catherine and Laurence Anholt

The right of Laurence and Catherine Anholt to be identified as
author and illustrator respectively of this work has been asserted by them
in accordance with the Copyright, Designs and Patents Act 1988

This book has been typeset in Bembo

Printed in China

British Library Cataloguing in Publication Data:
a catalogue record for this book is available from the British Library.

ISBN-13: 978-1-4063-0346-9
ISBN-10: 1-4063-0346-1

www.walkerbooks.co.uk

What Makes Me HAPPY?

Catherine and Laurence Anholt

WALKER BOOKS
AND SUBSIDIARIES
LONDON · BOSTON · SYDNEY · AUCKLAND

What makes me laugh?

tickly toes

a big red nose

being rude

silly food

acting crazy

my friend Maisie

What makes me cry?

wasps that sting

a fall from a swing

wobbly wheels

head over heels

What makes me bored?

Grown-ups...

moaning   groaning   eating   meeting   walking   talking

feeding   reading   sitting   knitting   stopping   shopping

What makes me pleased?

Look how much I've grown!

I can do it on my own!

What makes us jealous?

Her!

What makes me scared?

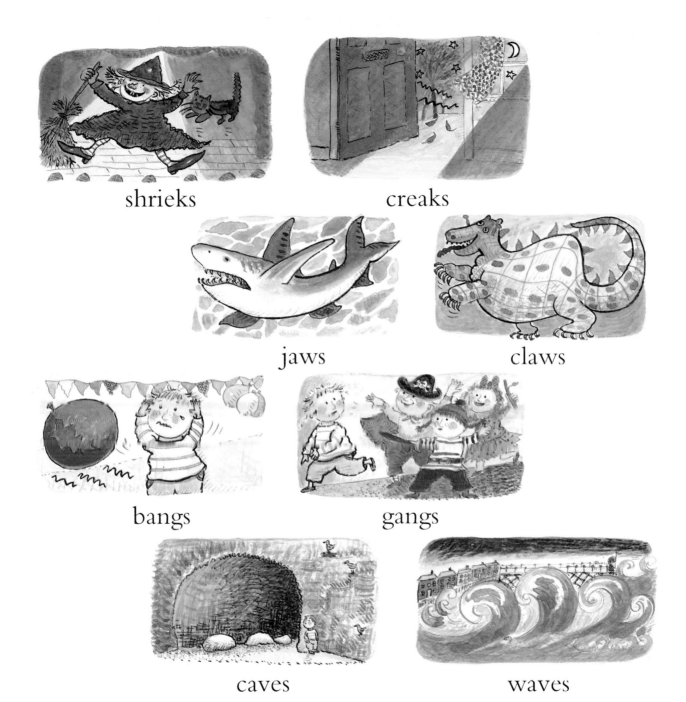

shrieks

creaks

jaws

claws

bangs

gangs

caves

waves

What makes me sad?

Rain, rain, every day.

No one wants to let me play.

Someone special's far away.

What makes us excited?

A roller-coaster ride

Here comes the bride!

The monster's on his way!

A party day

What makes me shy?

My first day

What makes me cross?

Days when buttons won't go straight
and I want to stay up late
and I hate what's on my plate...
Why won't anybody wait?

What makes us all happy?

making a castle

opening a parcel

singing a song

skipping along

windy weather

finding a feather and...

Being together.

WALKER BOOKS is the world's leading independent publisher of children's books. Working with the best authors and illustrators we create books for all ages, from babies to teenagers – books your child will grow up with and always remember. So…

FOR THE BEST CHILDREN'S BOOKS, LOOK FOR THE BEAR